THIS IS A BORZOI BOOK PUBLISHED BY ALFRED A. KNOPF

Copyright © 1999, 2001 by Hachette Livre
All rights reserved under International and Pan-American Copyright
Conventions. Published in the United States of America by Alfred A.
Knopf, a division of Random House, Inc., New York, and simultaneously in
Canada by Random House of Canada Limited, Toronto. Distributed by
Random House, Inc., New York. Originally published in France as Gaspard
et Lisa au musée by Hachette Jeunesse in 1999. KNOPF, BORZOI BOOKS,
and the colophon are registered trademarks of Random House, Inc.
www.randomhouse.com/kids
Library of Congress Cataloging-in-Publication Data
Gutman, Anne.
Gaspard and Lisa at the museum / Anne Gutman, Georg Hallensleben.
p.   cm.
Summary: While on a school field trip to the natural history museum,
Gaspard and Lisa have an exciting adventure in the dinosaur room.
ISBN 0-375-81117-6
[1. Museums—Fiction. 2. School field trips—Fiction.] I. Hallensleben,
Georg. II. Title.
PZ7.G9846 Gap 2001 [E]—dc21   00-062015
First Borzoi Books edition: September 2001
Printed in France: 10 9 8 7 6 5 4 3

Gaspard and Lisa at the Museum

ANNE GUTMAN · GEORG HALLENSLEBEN

w York

Yesterday we went on a class trip to the Museum of Natural History. We were very excited. "Gaspard and Lisa, please try to stay out of trouble," our teacher said as we got on the bus.

On the bus, our teacher told us about some of the animal exhibits that we would see. Lisa had been to the museum before, and she said there was something even better: dinosaurs so big

that one of their footprints could make a swimming pool for us.

The museum was very interesting.
Our teacher showed us everything:

butterflies,

monkeys,

tigers,

elephants,

and even the
skeleton of a whale.

But the exhibit of extinct animals was the most exciting. "Gaspard and Lisa," our classmates joked, "you look like extinct animals. The museum may want to keep you forever." Everyone laughed—except Lisa and me. But it gave me an idea.

"Lisa, let's play
a joke on our
classmates,"
I said, and I told
her my plan.

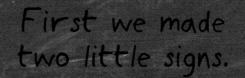

First we made two little signs.

Then we crept under the bars.

RARE LEOPARD
with white spots

We put the signs in front of us
and froze like statues.

I had forgotten to take off my scarf, but our classmates didn't notice. Some even took pictures of us . . .

. . . lots of pictures.

Our plan worked perfectly . . .

. . . so perfectly that our class left without us. The lights went out. The door closed. OH, NO! We were locked in the museum! "What's to become of us?" Lisa cried. "Don't be afraid," I answered. "We'll find something to eat, we'll go to sleep, and tomorrow we'll leave."

But the only thing to eat was dinosaur bones, and in the dark, they were sort of scary.

It was terrible being locked in the dark.
Suddenly, the dinosaur started growling.
GRRRRR! "HELP!" we shouted.

But it wasn't the dinosaur. It was the guard's dog, who came to rescue us. Our teacher and classmates were happy to see us—and, BOY, were we happy to see them!